Hello Kitty

I Love My
Daddy

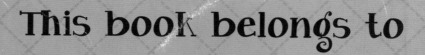

This book belongs to

······································

and my daddy is
the best ever!

© 1976, 2014 [UN]ADIO CO., LTD

First published in the UK by H[arperCollins] HarperCollins *Children's Books* in 2014

1 3 [...] 5 7 9 10 8 6 4 2

ISB[N]: 978-0-00-755940-4

Written by Neil Dunnicliffe
Designed by Wayne Redwood

Hello Kitty

I Love My
Daddy

HarperCollins *Children's Books*

Hello Kitty thinks
her daddy is the
best daddy ever.

He's funny and kind
and very brave!

Daddy works very hard...

but he also
loves to play!

Hello Kitty likes to
snuggle up with Daddy...

but when he snoozes,
his snores are very loud!

Daddy loves to cook Hello Kitty's
favourite foods...

but he's not too
good at clearing up!

Daddy likes to sing along
to his favourite songs...

but Hello Kitty likes it

when he stops!

When Hello Kitty is scared,

Daddy is always there.

If Hello Kitty is hurt...

Daddy will kiss it better.

Daddy can always solve it.

(Unless it's maths!)

Daddy always listens
to Hello Kitty.

They love to chat
about their days.

Daddy teaches Hello Kitty
lots of new things...

such as the
names of trees

and flowers
and stars,

and all
about football

and fast
cars too!

Daddy's cuddles are the cuddliest ever.

They make everything right in the world.

Daddy makes Hello Kitty
feel like a princess...

and she thinks he's as handsome
as a king!

At bedtime, Daddy reads
wonderful stories.

They make Hello Kitty
feel cosy and warm.

Hello Kitty loves her daddy very much...

and Daddy loves Hello Kitty very much too.

How much do you love your daddy?

The world of

Hello Kitty

Enjoy all of these wonderful Hello Kitty books.

Picture books

Where's Hello Kitty?

Activity books

...and more!

Hello Kitty and friends story book series